Fire Mate

To Florence Van de Water -

May your circle of all-oneness
always include a fire-mate for
your soul -

Sincerely, Olga Cossi

Fire Mate

By Olga Cossi

Photography by John McLaughlin, *Independent Coast Observer,* Gualala, California

Designed by Garry Hood

Independence Press, Independence, Missouri

Library of Congress Cataloging in Publication Data

Cossi, Olga.
  Fire mate.

  SUMMARY: An Indian girl searched for her fire
mate and finds it in a stray dog. Then the original
owner comes to claim the dog.
  [1. Indians of North America — Fiction.
2. Loneliness — Fiction] I. Title.
PZ7.C819FI   [Fic]   77-1334
ISBN 0-8309-0163-9

Printed in the United States of America

DEDICATION

To Ivan, the dreamer,
and my own fire mate.

CONTENTS

CHAPTER ONE

I am an Indian girl whose tribal name is Walakea. My American name is Yvonne. My family calls me Yvonne, but in the secret chambers of my heart I am Walakea.

Even though we live on a reservation near a big city, my people still remember many of their ancient legends. Sometimes they tell them to the children of the tribe. I am young and cannot know the true meaning of all the legends, yet there is one I know. This is the tradition of the Great One who is guardian of soul-fires. All Indians have soul-fires which they must share with fire mates to have light and warmth within the sacred circle of their being. Sometimes they must search for years to find their fire mates. Sometimes they must search throughout their lives. They know when they have found the right mates because their soul-fires burst into flame.

I-Yvonne was like any other girl on our reservation, busy playing and growing up. But I-Walakea was hungry for my fire mate.

I began looking among my brothers and sisters for the special one who was to share my flame. The one was not there.

Then I began searching among my friends, the other children on the reservation. Surely there must be another soul-fire like mine whose flame needed to be kindled. Still I could not find that one. All the other Indian children were busy feeding their own young flames as if they did not need a fire mate. But I did, so I kept looking—alone.

I went deep into the reservation forest which is my play yard. I learned to lie so still that the wild deer would come very close to me. I waited, but not one ever became friendly enough to be my fire mate. It was then I learned that man and beast have become separated by a wall of fear. Few have been able to find an opening through that wall or to rise over it. I found it between me and all the wildlife in my forest. The rabbits and raccoons, even the squirrels and playful chipmunks, let me come very close, but not close enough. The birds, too, accepted my presence in the forest, yet not one among their many kinds and colors would become the mate I was seeking to kindle my soul-fire.

During summer vacations there was much to do on our reservation because of the forest that surrounded us. I-Yvonne was too busy then to worry about such things as the legend of the soul-fire. I-Walakea was not thought of often. When winter came and storms kept us indoors, then even I-Yvonne felt the loneliness of Walakea. I spent many hours thinking about my fire mate. My family did not know why I was alone so much. They all seemed too busy tending their own flames to notice that my longing was deep and painful.

At last I spoke to my mother of my search. "I need a fire mate!" I cried out, my eyes lowered so she could not see how frightened I was to speak those words.

Out of the corner of my eye I could see Mother looking at me in wonder. The longing for a fire mate is an Indian secret. Now that my people live on reservations it is not often that children have this secret in their memory —or are brave enough to talk about it. After a long while Mother spoke. "I will go to my own soul-fire and ask wisdom for you."

Swiftly I raised my eyes to look at Mother. It was no use. She had "closed her face" as only an Indian can do. Her thoughts were safely hidden as if behind a mask. I ran outside before my own feelings began to show.

For two days I waited, watching Mother only when her face was turned away. The second morning as I awoke, she was standing by my bed. My sisters, with whom I share a bedroom, were still asleep. Mother dropped to her knees and motioned for me to be silent. When she spoke her eyes were soft and her voice low.

"You must go to the Great One for your fire mate. It is a path you will walk alone. It is not an easy path to find. Many before you have sought it and failed. The Great One is the Source of life and lives in all things. Nothing living is made to be lonely, but to be all-one. This is the true meaning of the word 'alone.' If you will go to the Great One you will be led to your fire mate, and your soul-fire will burst into flame. It will be as two wings beating together all in one motion, or two eyes seeing together all in one vision, or two halves of a circle coming together to form a whole. This is all-oneness—to be always alone and yet never lonely."

Mother's voice fell silent, but her eyes were still speaking. They were asking me if I understood. I did not, yet I could not tell her this. I could feel Mother reading my eyes.

"I will go to the Great One," I whispered quickly, sounding as grown-up as I could. "But where will I find this One?"

"Only remember to listen well, and you will know," Mother replied. "Remember, listen well, my daughter, my brave Walakea who is called Yvonne." With that she touched her lips to my forehead and was gone.

All that day at school I thought of what Mother had said. When the bus took us back to the reservation I played in the forest alone where I could listen better. No word came. Was I to go to some special place before the Great One would speak? Was there a sacred ground I must find, a high mountain I must climb first? I wondered, but I would not speak to Mother again. So I played in the forest until evening, waiting and listening.

Soon after dinner Mother sent us children to bed, for the school bus came early in the morning. My brothers and sisters were all older than I, so even though they went to their rooms, they brought books with them to read in bed. I lingered near Father's chair as I said good-night. I wondered if he knew where the Great One was. How I longed to ask him! But because I was Walakea as well as Yvonne, I closed my face Indian fashion and said nothing. Only with my eyes did we speak, my father and I, and Mother's eyes joined us. Their soul-fires must be well matched to cause such a warm flame as I felt there between them, I noted silently.

Later in my bed my longing was more painful than ever. My two sisters' beds were across the room from mine, but we could have been moons apart. They had their books and each other. I knew they considered me too young to share their conversation. If only

I could have shared with them my secret longing for a fire mate!

"Oh, Great One," I spoke inwardly, "you who are all-knowing must understand how I-Walakea feel even though I-Yvonne hide it! Surely you must know that although I am only a girl child I have a soul-fire which waits to be kindled! Surely you must know who and where my fire mate is!"

I gathered my pillow in my arms and dug my face into its softness, but the loneliness did not go away. I wanted so much to run to Mother or Father and crawl into the safe circle of their arms as I had done as a small child. Yet if I was big enough to seek a fire mate of my own, I must be big enough to do so alone, as Mother said. So I lay back and listened.

One by one the lights in the bedrooms were turned off until the house was in silent darkness. Still sleep did not come. Outside the moon was shining, casting a pale light through the open window. "That's where I should be," I told myself, "out in the forest where our people lived before they learned to shut themselves in houses made with thick walls. . . . Let there be no walls between us, O Great One!" I prayed.

Softly I slipped from my bed and changed into warm clothing. I carried my shoes in my arms and silently made my way through the house to the back door. In a moment

I was outdoors, looking up at the stars,
letting the light of the moon wash my face.

The forest I knew so well seemed vast
and new under the veil of night. Of course
I was not afraid. I knew my friends the wild
creatures were as busy at night as we Indian
children were during the day. Although I
could not see or hear them, they were there,
probably watching me from their hiding
places.

My shoes crunched on the dry leaves as
I followed the road which the reservation bus
took each day to and from school. It was
easy walking so I set a brisk pace. Out here
I could listen better for the Great One
who surely must answer me soon. The road
wound through tall trees standing side by
side like sleeping men wrapped in robes made
of leaves. Although my eyes were busy
looking into the shadows which pressed all
around me, my ears were listening for the
voice that must come. Would the Great One
face me in a sudden burst of light or with
the sound of rolling thunder as Indian drums
calling? I wondered as I walked, but I was not
afraid. Because the animals were safe in the
forest, so was I.

It seemed only a short time before I came
to the end of the reservation road. Here it
joined the paved highway to the city. I had
traveled these five miles to and from school
many times in the bus, yet this night I was

seeing the forest for the first time. Surely it must be the home of the Great One I was seeking! Was not this vast dome of stars meant for the pleasure of the One whose idea it was? So I walked on in silence, listening.

I-Walakea remembered as I walked. One by one I recalled the tribal legends I had heard. I recounted to myself the lives of the brave men and women whose deeds had blazed a trail in Indian history that would never be lost nor forgotten. I knew their greatness and strength had come from within, from the hearth of a soul-fire that had been kindled. What had made those soul-fires catch and burn with a blaze of glory? Did the Great One choose those few to whom a fire mate would be given? Or was it the brave leaders themselves who chose to listen and thus were guided to the all-oneness that sparked the eternal flame?

I heard no answer to my questions, but as the memories flowed a quiet and sure sense of peace filled my being. It was as if remembering had laid the kindling of my soul-fire. It needed only to be touched to burst into living flame.

Suddenly a flash of light lit the treetops in the distance. Could it be the lights of the city so soon, I wondered? Then I caught the sound of a motor whining. A car was coming. From the sound I could tell it was being driven at high speed. I watched the headlights flash through the trees. The car was getting close. I ran across the road and hid in the shadows of the thick brush that bordered it, waiting and watching.

Now the car was very close. Instead of racing past me, it seemed to be slowing down! Then the wheels spun to a stop in the loose gravel on the shoulder of the road.

The motor was still running when the front door on my side swung open. A shaft of light lit the interior of the car. I saw two men. They were arguing. The man nearest me was carrying a bundle that looked like a feed sack.

"Put an end to him!" the driver yelled.

"We don't have to worry about that!" the man with the bundle snapped back. "He can't get out of the sack by himself. And who is there to find him out here?"

"Don't waste time arguing—ditch him, and let's get going before another car comes by. It could happen...even out here!" the driver said.

The man with the bundle swore as he jumped out of the car. I swallowed hard....He was running toward the very bushes where I was hiding! I could almost reach out and touch him as he pushed past me and dumped the bundle on the ground with a thud.

"Come on!" the driver was yelling. But the second man was already on his way back to the car. The motor roared, and they were gone.

I stood there shivering as the car spun away. Then I looked at the sack. Even in the shadowy light of the moon I could see the burlap moving. Whatever was inside was alive. I pushed my way to the sack. I had to open it!

Kneeling on the ground I worked the knot loose. The open end began to move. I stepped back and waited. There was a great wave of motion in the burlap. Then a head appeared, a white head with a black-masked face. It was a small dog. I stepped closer. The puppy looked like a ball of fur — mostly white, with some darker spots. And such eyes! They were as big as my own felt as I stood there staring. Before I could recover from my surprise, the puppy gave a happy wiggle and crawled toward me. I dropped to my knees and he lunged clumsily into my arms.

I had never felt anything so soft in my life! Not even the newly hatched chicks my parents raised were as silky. My heart was still pounding so loudly I could not think. Then a wet tongue kissed my cheek. Without warning, my soul-fire burst into flame!

I knelt there, letting the pup nuzzle me, feeling as if my chest could not hold the warm glow swelling inside. Was this the fire mate I had come seeking?

As if to answer, the pup kissed me again and again. There was no mistaking the fresh burst of flame I felt. If I had not been here, I reasoned, the pup would not have been found in time. We had needed each other, this very night, and here we were—together. That was enough for me to know. I stood up, stretching as tall as my nine years would let me. I searched the sky high above the trees. I could see nothing but stars. I was alone, yet all at once I understood what Mother meant when she had spoken of all-oneness. I said the only words that came: "Thank you, O Great One!" Then I knelt and gathered the puppy in my arms.

"What is your name, fire mate?" I asked the soft face so close to mine. "What are you called? Why did those men want to destroy you?" The puppy's only answer was more wiggles and a kiss.

I knew this was no time for questions, not with the long road home ahead of me. It would not be easy, in spite of my happy heart. The puppy was heavy and so soft he kept slipping through my arms. I tried to let him walk by himself, but his legs were so short that he could not crawl over rough ground. I dared not walk on the pavement even though it would have been much easier. I chose to stay in the shadows on the edge of the underbrush just in case a car should come by. So I walked on, stopping often to rest my arms.

Once I got back to the reservation road

I felt much safer. By then the moon had swung directly overhead and a breeze was blowing. I wondered if my forest friends saw me and were curious about my fire mate. Surely they could hear me talking to him when we stopped to rest. Would they accept this puppy as a natural part of the forest as they had accepted me?

After many stops we came to the clearing where the tribal houses stood in a half-circle. Our house was small and near the woods, because my parents were poor; but our yard was swept clean, and not even the best or biggest house had a better garden than ours.

How good it was to turn into our drive-way! I was suddenly very tired. I sat on the porch steps and rested while the puppy wandered about—but never far from my feet. I had to remember everything that had happened, I decided. Someday my story might be told as an Indian legend. Not one moment of it must be forgotten. So I remembered as I rested.

At last I gathered the puppy into my arms and slipped quietly inside. I left my shoes by the door and walked noiselessly to the room I shared with my sisters. I could hear them breathing deeply as they slept. I laid the puppy in the middle of my bed while I undressed. He was just settling himself into a ball when I climbed in beside him.

What a feeling it was to lie there and run

my fingers through the silky coat of the fire mate I had searched for so long! Warmer than the blankets was the glow of all-oneness which seemed to fill the room. In the morning I would tell Mother of my night search and show her my fire mate. And in the morning the puppy must be named! With that thought I drifted off to sleep.

CHAPTER TWO

When I opened my eyes, Mother was standing by my bed. She looked from me to the pup and back again. Not a word did she speak with her lips, but she looked at me knowingly and I was sure my soul-fire was reflected in my eyes. My hand was still resting on the soft ball of fur by my side. I tried to keep my face closed, but my smile would not stay hidden completely.

Mother's eyes were not smiling, but they were soft. She motioned for me to follow her. I tried not to wake the pup as I picked him up and followed her down the hall. She led me into the small bedroom that was hers and Father's. Here a lamp was lit. Father was dressing for work. He stood still for a moment as we entered, then his eyes flew to Mother's face. I thought it best for me not to interfere while their eyes

spoke to each other, so I sat on the edge of
their bed and laid the puppy on my lap.
Father and Mother joined me, sitting one on
each side.

"Tell us how you got this dog, Yvonne,"
Father spoke quietly.

As briefly as I could I told how I had
felt the need for a fire mate so strongly
that I had gone out into the night where I
could listen better. I told how the memory
of our legends and the stories of Indian
leaders had made me feel brave and sure that
the Great One would not let my listening
fail. I explained about the speeding car and
the two men, how I had hidden in the bushes,
and how the sack had been thrown almost at
my feet. I could sense their excitement as I told
about opening the sack and watching the
white head and black-masked face appear
out of the burlap folds. Then I paused.

"Go on, Yvonne," Father urged.

I chose my words carefully as I told of the
puppy's kiss and the instant flaming of my
soul-fire. I turned to Mother. "It was then that
I understood the all-oneness you had spoken
of, and I thanked the Great One for this
gift of gifts."

For a moment neither parent spoke. Then
Father asked, "Was it not foolish for you,
a young girl, to go out into the forest alone
at night?"

"But the wild animals live there, and they

are safe," I explained. "Surely the forest is the home of the Great One even at night."

Now it was Mother's turn to question. "How far would you have walked if that car had not come along?"

"Until I got my answer from the Great One as you said I would. Now Walakea is not alone anymore. Now she is all-one with her fire mate."

The pup in my arms sighed in his sleep as if he too understood the secret meaning of all-oneness. I stroked his fur and felt again the wonder of that inner flame.

For a moment Mother and Father talked together with their eyes. "Let me see him," Father requested.

I scooped up the furry ball in my lap and handed it to Father. His face became soft as he felt the tender body and looked into the round, innocent eyes that opened sleepily. A light wiggle let Father know that his attention was welcome. He examined the pup carefully.

"This is a valuable dog, Yvonne," he began. "I do not know the breed, but a pup this size with a coat like this doesn't just happen. Which means those men must have stolen him. That would explain why he was being dumped. We'll have to take him to the police."

The police! Without thinking I grabbed the pup from Father's hands and buried my face in his fur. How my soul-fire flickered at those words! What if the police should take him from me! "He is mine!" I cried. "I told you the truth! He was meant for me, and I for him! What if the police take him away from me?"

Mother's voice was as calm as her eyes when she spoke. "If what you understand of all-oneness is true, then if the pup is your fire mate he will not be taken from you, will he? We must trust the soul-fire to the One who lights it. Father's words are wise, and we must do the wise thing. Surely the Great One would not expect less of us. The police must be told the truth."

There was no doubting the wisdom of Mother's words. My fears were calmed. Then Father spoke again. "Walakea must remember that the Indian legends are told and retold to make us brave enough to do right, not brave enough to do wrong." He was not looking at me as he spoke. He seemed to be looking far into the past, perhaps remembering how important legends were to our people since they had retreated to the reservations.

"What is right, Yvonne, for all concerned, not just for you? If the pup is stolen, what about the people from whom he was taken? And those two men, should not the police be told what you saw and heard so they can try to catch the men and stop them from doing even greater wrong?" Father asked.

The thought of someone else claiming my fire mate made the flame of my soul-fire waver. "The pup is mine!" I repeated. "It was the Great One who brought us together! This is my fire mate forever!"

Father's voice was gentle but firm as he replied, "But if the thought of someone taking this puppy from you makes you so sad, how must his owners feel who could be searching for him even now?"

How I wanted to shut out the rightness of Father's words! Mother saw the pain in my eyes and spoke. "The Great One does not work with evil, but with good. Evil is but an empty space to be filled. Fill it now with trust. Only in this way can you keep securely and not lose the good you have been given."

"Even if the pup has been stolen, when his owners are found perhaps we can buy him and he will be yours honestly," Father added.

"But they might not want to sell him! Or he could cost many more dollars than we can pay! He is a fine dog, even as you said, Father," I argued.

Mother answered quickly, "Walakea, will not the One who guided you to the right place to find and save this bit of life last night guide you now just as surely to the right way to keep him?"

I could not answer, for her words were true.

"There is no time to go to the police station now," Father decided, "because I must go to work and you must be getting ready for school. But tonight after supper we will go."

"And now we will have breakfast," Mother said. "Go wake your brothers and sisters, Yvonne, and show them what you found. I will get Father fed and off to work."

When I reached my bedroom, my sisters were already whispering together for they had heard us talking. I placed the still sleeping puppy in the middle of my blankets. My sisters sat straight up in bed, their eyes wide with wonder. Then they threw back the covers and came running over.

"Yvonne, baby, where did you get that dog?" my sister Margaret asked, rubbing the pup's soft coat. "My gosh, what is he made of? What kind of dog is he? How did he get here? Whose is he?" She asked questions without waiting for answers.

I warmed my words by my soul-fire before I spoke. "He is mine," I replied simply.

"Did you steal him? And where would you find such a dog to steal?" Margaret teased.

My oldest sister Leona gave Margaret a playful poke. "Silly, Yvonne isn't old enough to steal! But Yvonne, baby, where *did* you get him? He's just beautiful!" Her hands caressed the pup who rolled over, exposing a broad empty belly begging to be rubbed.

"He is mine!" I repeated. More fierce than pride was the bond I felt toward my fire mate. Yet how could I explain this to someone who had not waited for that flame to come to life within her?

Mother rescued me from further questions. She stepped quickly into our room and scooped up the pup in one practiced motion. "The question isn't, 'How did he get here?' but 'How are you girls going to get to school unless you catch the bus?' Right now this little one needs to be fed, and you bigger ones need to get dressed so you can be fed too. Come dress quickly now . . . *quickly!*"

In the hurried preparation that followed, I had only a few minutes alone with my fire mate before it was time to run for the bus. Instantly my flame responded to his nearness! Mother caught my eye as I hugged the bundle of fur one last time. "He will be well taken care of until you return," her glance said. I knew this to be true. Still when I-Yvonne stepped aboard the school bus that morning, I-Walakea stayed behind with my fire mate. Somehow the teacher put up with my half-presence that day without scolding me.

When school was out, I was first in line for the return ride home. How long those five miles seemed! Finally the bus stopped at our house and I was running up the walk to greet a lively puppy. My brothers and sisters joined in the happy reunion, but there was no doubt that I was the one the pup was waiting for. When the play got too rough, that wiggling ball of affection came running to me for comfort. My soul-fire burned brightly as the puppy made himself at home between my ankles as if they were his special hiding place!

Many times I was asked where the dog came from or how I had gotten him. Always I answered simply, "He is mine," and said no more.

As usual my oldest brother Paul had important things on his mind so the mystery did not keep him interested for long. My brother Clyde was Paul's shadow. They left together for the privacy of their upstairs room. Margaret and Leona soon went looking for Mother to ask her the questions they saw I was avoiding. So the puppy and I were left alone.

Never for a moment the remainder of that afternoon were my fire mate and I separated.

We ran errands together. We explored the edge of the forest behind our house together. But mostly we played together. Mother noticed my happiness. Twice she joined us in our play, letting the pup tug at her sleeve or chew on her fingers as he growled in mock anger. The all-oneness I felt was like a ring of light that touched everyone who came within its reach. When Father arrived home just before dark and I remembered that we must go to the police station, even this did not dull the happiness I felt. Over and over I said to myself, "I-Walakea have found my fire mate." And there he was to prove it!

No sooner had we finished eating than Father put on his jacket and told my brothers and sisters where we were going. Mother assigned the kitchen chores; then she too slipped into a jacket and prepared to leave. There was little protest from my brothers and sisters, for a chance to be home alone was even more tempting than curiosity about their little sister's dog.

We drove the five miles to the city in silence. I had the pup's warm body pressed against me to keep my soul-fire burning brightly and ward off fears of facing the police. Chief Garret greeted Father and Mother at the door of the police station.

"Good evening, Joe, and Mrs. Laiwa," the chief said. He nodded to me as he noticed the pup I was carrying. "What have we here?"

Without mentioning the Indian legend or the reason for my walk that night, Father told Chief Garret my story. "Yvonne wants to keep the puppy, but she also wants to do what is right, so here we are," he finished.

"May I see the pup?" the officer asked. How cold my soul-fire became as I handed him that soft bundle!

"Hum," Chief Garret murmured as he

examined the pup inch by inch. "Looks
to me as if you have a purebred Saint
Bernard here. Could be about six to eight
weeks old. Probably pedigreed with a
coat like this and these markings. And look
at the size of that head. . . and feet! He's
a beauty." He paused, then looked directly
at me as he continued. "This is very likely
a valuable dog, stolen and dumped because
he was 'hot.' By 'hot' I mean the law was
breathing down those men's necks and they
had to get rid of the evidence of their crime."

Father and Mother exchanged glances but
said nothing. How hard it was to trust at that
moment! I wanted to snatch my pup from
Chief Garret's arms and run and hide in the
forest forever. But my parents' faces were
closed, and I must do my best to close mine.

"I'll do some checking," Chief Garret was
continuing, "but meanwhile all we can do is
wait for a bulletin on a stolen dog to come in.
I'll keep the pup here until. . ."

"No!" Father interrupted. "Our daughter
will keep the dog until. . . in case the owner is
found."

Chief Garret must have seen the feeling
in my eyes I could not keep hidden. "If the
pup is not claimed, young lady, he's yours,"
he began. "But there is a good chance that
this pup is worth searching for, even if he
was transported a long distance. You know,
he could have been stolen across the state

line, since it's only three hundred miles away."

"If his owners are found," Father explained, "we want to buy the dog."

"His price could be pretty high," Chief Garret replied. He lifted the pup in his hands as if they were scales, and his eyes twinkled. "Some breeders sell their Saint Bernard pups by the pound, and this one could weight close to twenty! That would mean several hundred dollars, at least."

I looked at my parents' faces, but there was no sign of what even one hundred dollars could mean to our family.

"If he is for sale we will buy him," Father repeated seriously.

Chief Garret looked at me with soft eyes. "I hope for your sake, young lady, that it works out that way." He handed me the pup. "What did you say your name was?"

"I am called Yvonne, but my Indian name is Walakea," I said between the puppy's happy kisses.

"Now then, Yvonne Walakea, I want you to tell me as much as you can about those two men and their car," the Police Chief said.

As best I could remember, I described what I had seen and heard the night before. When Chief Garret was satisfied with the details of my story he laid down his pen and stood up. "I have just one more question to ask. What were you doing walking along the highway alone at night? Were you by any chance running away from home?"

"Oh, no!" I answered quickly. Then I paused. What reason could I give? I looked at my parents and knew I must tell the truth. "I-Walakea was listening for the voice of the Great One who is guardian of the soul-fires of our people," I explained.

"I see," Chief Garret replied, his face denying his words. "I hope you don't do that very often."

"Oh, no! Just once. I found my answer," I continued, my eyes on the fire mate I was holding close.

Chief Garret scuffed his feet on the floor and turned back to his desk. "Well, thank you, Yvonne Walakea, for coming to us and telling about your experience. Somewhere someone must be searching for this pup and hoping he will be found and reported. No matter what happens from now on, you have done the right thing." The Chief shook my hand before continuing. "I do suggest one more thing. Take that pup to a vet as soon as you can and make sure he is in good health. And find out about the breed. Saint Bernards need special food and care. I had one of my own once when I was a boy. We grew up together. That's a lot of dog for a young girl, but you two look like a good match for each other."

I felt my soul-fire spark at his words. Then Chief Garret continued. "Tomorrow is

Saturday. Suppose I come by in the morning;
you can show me where you were hiding,
and we can look for that sack. It may help
in identifying the men, or at least give us
a clue as to where they were from. Then
I'll drive you to the vet's and we'll see what he
says about the pup. Would that be all right,
Mrs. Laiwa? Could you come with us?"

Mother looked at Father as she spoke.
"That would be fine."

"How about nine or ten o'clock, then?"
Chief Garret asked.

Again Mother consented. Father and Chief
Garret shook hands and we left.

CHAPTER THREE

*T*he next morning I got up when Father went to work. After breakfast I took the puppy for a run in the forest. How he gloried in the freedom of my play yard! Too soon Mother called, and we got ready for Chief Garret's arrival. He was right on time. I felt both fear and pride as we drove off in the police car. Our people have not always been treated honorably by the law, so we accepted with gratitude Chief Garret's genuine interest.

When we reached the end of the reservation road, the chief parked the car and we walked along the edge of the clearing as I had done two nights before. Very soon the underbrush became dense. I knew this must be where I had hidden. The three of us searched while the puppy tried his best to keep up with us. I was the first to spot the sack and called Chief Garret. He picked it

up carefully and carried it back to his car.
Then he returned, bringing a camera. He
searched the ground on the shoulder of the
road where he found a set of tire tracks
undisturbed. After studying them, he took a
few pictures. We walked back to the car
in silence.

In a few minutes we arrived at the
veterinarian's office, a Dr. White whom Chief
Garret recommended highly. In the waiting
room the pup was a magnet. Everyone
wanted to pet him and feel his silky coat.
Dr. White confirmed Chief Garret's statement
that the pup was a Saint Bernard — and
probably a pedigreed dog. The doctor pointed
out the pup's short nose and broad skull,
the straight back and strong rear — sure
signs that he was a good Saint Bernard and
a valuable dog. Of course I already knew the
puppy's value. I had felt it the night we
found each other.

At last the examination was over. Dr. White
gave Mother a written diet for the pup and
made an appointment for a later visit if he
was not claimed. Quickly my heart claimed
him as my fire mate. No matter what Chief
Garret or Dr. White or anyone said, the Great
One had sent him to me. He was mine. I
would not let the fear of losing him threaten
the flame he had kindled.

Soon we were home again and I was free
to take the puppy into the forest. Here it

was cool and silent and I could listen to the inner feeling of all-oneness which was waiting to spill over. Besides, the time had come for me to give my fire mate a name. Surely the One who had sent him to me would reveal it. Just as I was Walakea, so my fire mate had a name that belonged to him. I would wait to know it.

When we reached a little meadow, I threw myself down on the warm grass and let the puppy climb over me. We tumbled and rolled, and when we tired, I led him to the small stream that ran down a shallow gully. We drank together of the clear, sweet water. Then the puppy stretched out to sleep. I sat on a rock and watched the water dancing and swirling in terraced pools as it made its way downstream.

What *was* water, I wondered. Was it like thinking which flowed naturally in streams made of words? Surely the very words "fire mate" caused my mind to dance happily just as the water at my feet was doing. Yes, and the word "police" had been like a huge boulder which dammed my happiness. It took much thinking to rise above the deep pool of fear that word left in my mind.

A name was really just a word, I decided. When I was called by the name "Walakea" I thought of myself as an Indian princess, child of the great One who ruled the forest I played in. But when I was called "Yvonne"

I became just a little sister on a lonely reservation.

I looked at the sleeping puppy and wondered what I should name him. After a few moments I felt the need to speak out. "Oh, Great One, giver of the all-oneness I know, by what word do you call the fire mate here at my feet?" Then I lay back beside the puppy and slept.

"Zoll!" I awoke with a start as I heard the name spoken. I looked around. I was alone, except for the pup at my side, yet I heard the name "Zoll" spoken plainly. It is a good name, I thought, pleased by its sound. And so my fire mate was named.

I roused Zoll and urged him to follow me home. I would tell Mother of the naming. But first I paused a moment and said "Thank you!" Who can guess what broad rivers of joy flow from such sacred words!

My brothers and a group of friends were playing football on the street in front of our house as we turned down the road. How excited Zoll became at their running and shouting! Several stopped playing when they saw him and came to join us. Soon we were surrounded by noisy boys. My brother Paul got down on his knees and started a mock battle with Zoll. The pup faced the challenge with flashing teeth and a happy growl. The other boys were shouting encouragement to Zoll, but in his rushing he got off balance and

bumped his muzzle against Paul's shoe.
Quickly Zoll gathered his feet under him and
retreated to his favorite hiding place between
my legs.

"Go forward, Zoll!" I thought. "You have
nothing to fear." As if I had spoken aloud,
he ran forward to charge my brother's ankles.
Had he heard or felt my thoughts, I wondered?
I was beginning to discover that between fire
mates communication is as natural as the
flow of the stream in our forest.

CHAPTER FOUR

As Zoll grew, the silent bond between us grew also. Each day we ran farther in the woods, exploring the canyon walls and the freedom of open space. Sometimes I would shout as an Indian warrior, swinging to the top of a tree as I saw the grey squirrels do. From the ground Zoll would bark at me, a deep, full tone that sounded as if it came from a cave. But mostly we kept our voices silent and let our soul-fires communicate with growing confidence.

Chief Garret returned twice that first week to check on Zoll and report that no word had been received about a stolen Saint Bernard. Each time I saw the police car drive up my confidence wavered. Quickly I would recall Mother's words that the One who lit that inner flame would guard it as well, and my peace would return.

Chief Garret was as pleased as we were over Zoll's growth. Father had fashioned a brush from the dry head of a wild teasel for Zoll's thick coat. The bracts served as a comb as well as brush, keeping the silky hair as sleek as doeskin. Each day Zoll's beauty grew with his size. Chief Garret seemed as pleased as I.

Others were noticing Zoll too. The children on the reservation began finding excuses to come to our house and play with him. On our visits to Dr. White's office, many saw Zoll's beauty and could not look away. Children and parents alike asked to touch his coat as if it were a good luck charm that would somehow rub off on them. Zoll enjoyed the attention, lapping it up as a thirsty fawn drinking from a stream. But when I thought he had had enough, our soul-fires communicated instantly and he would come stand in his chosen place between my feet.

To help pay for the cost of Zoll's special food and visits to Dr. White, I agreed to work for my parents one hour each afternoon. Father was clearing land for a larger vegetable garden. My job was to walk back and forth over the newly turned earth and pick up rocks. These I stacked along the edge for a fence. As I worked, Zoll walked beside me. He could have slept in the shade, but he chose to stay at my side, helping me with his presence. During that hour we practiced letting our soul-fires talk. Or at least I practiced. To Zoll such communication seemed natural. He knew when a rock was too heavy and I must stop to rest. He knew when I became thirsty and would walk with me to the faucet. Together we drank and rested, and together we went back to the field.

Our walks in the forest became deep explorations as Zoll's legs grew strong enough to carry him greater distances. We found the headspring that fed the stream which ran down the gully on its way to the river. Many times we found deer and coon drinking here in the late afternoon. At first they were fearful of Zoll and fled, but soon they became part of our circle of silent communication and let us drink with them.

Zoll's attitude toward the forest beasts was a constant surprise. He could never under-stand their fear of him. I taught Zoll to approach the headspring from the lee side so his dog scent would not startle the other animals before they recognized us. Once we were seen, there would be a brief battle between the wild animal's eyes and his instincts. Those eyes had seen us many times and knew us as fellow creatures, but the instinct to fear our tame scent was equally present. Motionless Zoll and I would stand, letting our soul-fires communicate until we knew it was all right to move forward again.

Long after we were accepted at the spring, I often felt Zoll's puppy urge to play with those creatures. He wanted to run *with* the deer, not *after* them. Perhaps someday that would happen. For now we had to be content that we were allowed to share the cool water with those whose right to live here wild and free had no reservations.

As Zoll grew out of puppyhood, the bed we shared seemed to grow smaller. Once he accidentally rolled off the edge of the bed while turning over during the night. From then on he slept in the middle of the bed with his body pressed against mine. Fortunately my growth was slow, so I could give him the extra room he needed. Zoll meant "giving" for Mother too, because he made extra work for her which I now shared gladly. Mother knew as well as I the change that had come over Yvonne since Walakea had found her fire mate and the meaning of all-oneness. I worked willingly at whatever she asked of me and often before she asked. I was a whole person now, full of my own fulfillment, so I had much to give.

Summer vacation came in June and with it long lazy days in our forest. Occasionally I had to share Zoll's time with my brothers and sisters—but never his soul-fire. In this

we were as one. My brother Clyde had
always wanted an Indian pony of his own,
and Zóll was as close to that wish as he ever
came. Father taught Clyde how to use a
lariat. Zoll obliged by playing the part of a
wild pony. How swiftly he ran, his silky
white coat blowing like a silvery mane! Sometimes he was "tamed" or "broken" and
would pull their make-believe wagon or carry
secret messages hidden in the thick hair
on his back.

Although Zoll was now almost the size
of a small pony, Dr. White had warned us
never to ride him or put weight on his
hind quarters. A Saint Bernard's bones need
to carry his heavy body, the kindly
veterinarian explained. A young Saint can be
seriously hurt if he is forced to carry a greater
burden than is natural. It was enough for my
brothers, however, that Zoll looked and acted
like a pony. They were far too proud of
his swift beauty to risk hurting him. Besides,
it was more of a challenge to have to run
with a pony rather than *on* him, expecially if
that pony could turn into a fierce lion if
anything threatened!

Only once did another boy start a fight
with my brothers while Zoll was in sight. This
boy had a bad temper. As his anger rose,
so did his fists. He struck my brother Paul,
but before he could strike again Zoll charged
him. The boy saw that Saint Bernard mouth

open like a dark cave. He put out his hands
to ward off the charge, and Zoll "swallowed"
the boy's arms almost to the elbows, holding
them firmly trapped in his fleshy jowls.
When I had recovered from shock enough to
command Zoll to let go, the boy's arms were
slowly released and he pulled them out
one at a time. Only damp skin and a few
red pressure marks showed where the jaws
had clamped. From then on no one in my
family was ever threatened while Zoll was near.

Often on his day off Chief Garret drove up
to see Zoll. The police car came to mean
fun rather than fear. Like Dr. White, the
chief was proud to be one of Zoll's friends.
He liked to brush him until his coat gleamed,
and Zoll responded by waving his plume
tail and looking at his friend with those square
red eyes. Chief Garret explained that these
were the mark of a good Saint Bernard.

"He's the most beautiful Saint Bernard
I've ever seen!" the chief announced on one
of his visits. "Of course I'm not a professional
judge, but he looks like a winner to me.
Someday you should show him, Yvonne."

For a moment pride rose in my heart.
I could imagine the applause as I led Zoll
into the winner's circle. But could that blaze
of fame match the inner warmth of a soul-
fire? The silent voice inside me shouted
"No!" I had been given the gift of all-oneness
with my fire mate. Could I want more?

CHAPTER FIVE

*W*hen summer was over the
thought of going to school
began to worry me. How
could I leave Zoll and the forest for so
many hours? What would I learn in school
that I must know? Could the world of books
teach me more than the world of trees
and water, mountains and fields, summer sun
and winter storms? Would school kindle my
soul-fire or subdue it? I knew I could not
ask these questions of another. I could ask
only the Great One and he answered in
silence.

I noticed Mother's eyes following me
closely one day, and I sensed she knew of
my struggle to leave Zoll and the forest. I
was not surprised when she approached me
that afternoon. She spoke with calm
assurance. ''Zoll will be my companion when
you go back to school. We will learn to

understand each other, and that is good. Perhaps we can even walk in the forest, which I have not visited for so long."

Of course her words were right. Zoll and Mother *would* be good for each other! A sudden burst of happiness kindled my soul-fire and seemed to warm all three of us at once. I patted Zoll's head and smiled. I was ready for school.

It was not easy to leave him that first day, but what a welcome I got when the bus drove up in front of our house that afternoon! Now Zoll became as my shadow, staying closely beside me.

Until winter storms arrived Zoll and I always spent my first after-school hour in the forest, seeking and finding new trails or following old ones to see what changes had occurred. I still worked in the garden for an hour before supper, since Zoll's food was costing more than ever. When I did my homework at night, Zoll kept his eyes focused on my face, as if he could read there the lessons I saw on the pages of my school books.

So the months came and went until Zoll had been with us a full year. He was now more than half-grown, with a strong frame and heavy body. His chest was like a big white cloud; his back was straight and broad. Hours of running up the steep banks of the canyon wall had given his hind legs the

muscles they needed to carry his weight
with grace and ease.

I too had grown, especially in confidence
now that the bond between my fire mate
and me had become as natural as breathing.
My family had come to accept us as one,
so strong was our silent exchange of feelings.
Through Zoll I had learned to really listen.
Often I found myself knowing what someone
was going to say before it was said. I heard
it plainly, just as Zoll heard my thoughts
and responded to them. The circle of our
all oneness grew to include those we loved
until our seeing and our knowing often
blended.

One morning in early spring our school
hummed with excitement over an Easter
Festival to be held in the city the following
month. Posters were hung in the hallways;
my brother brought me to see them during
lunch hour. A pet show was one of the big
events planned. Among the awards there was
to be a cash prize for "best dog." Paul
and Clyde were sure the prize money was as
good as mine, since no other dog could be
better than Zoll!

It was not hard for them to convince
me. I could use the prize money to pay for
the new collar and license Father had just
bought, and for the special diet Dr. White
wanted Zoll kept on for at least another year.
A pet show sounded much easier than

picking up rocks in the garden or pulling weeds. Besides, it would be a chance to test Zoll's beauty against others.

There was lively conversation around our table that night as we told Mother and Father about the Easter Festival and the show. Father was quick to point out that such shows were won not only on beauty but also on performance in the ring. Zoll and I would have to practice many hours if we were to win. I knew Zoll would do instantly whatever I thought. It was I who must be trained, I decided, not him.

"Where can I learn what we must do?" I asked Father.

"Dr. White will surely know about pet shows. And if he doesn't Chief Garret should. Remember he had a Saint Bernard of his own when he was a boy," Father replied.

Soon Father and Mother drove Zoll and me down to see Dr. White and Chief Garret. Both were pleased to hear of the dog show and promised to do all they could to prepare Zoll for the event. Dr. White explained to Father how to build a simple practice ring with ropes and stakes. Once it was built, Chief Garret would come up on his day off and work with Zoll and me.

The next few weeks were filled with new activity. Zoll and I still ran in the forest each day as soon as I got home from school, but later we worked in the ring. It was not really work. Once I knew what to do, Zoll followed my lead without a word being spoken. Chief Garret marveled at the way we moved as one. To him it was a clever performance by a girl and her dog. To Zoll and me it was just being fire mates and sharing the same inner flame.

CHAPTER SIX

*W*hen the day came for the show I dressed in an Indian blouse Mother had beaded for me. She tied my braids with matching ribbons. My brothers helped brush Zoll with the teasel head until his coat bristled with electricity. Father had woven a leash of leather strips he dyed the same color as my blouse. Margaret loaned me her turquoise bracelet to wear, and Leona wiped the dust off our car. My family wanted me to be a credit to our people. When it was time to drive into town, I was seated in front with Mother and Father while my brothers and sisters crowded in the back with Zoll.

The pet show was being held in the high school auditorium. Chief Garret was there waiting for us, and so was Dr. White. The excitement began to mount. I wondered if I could listen for the Great One while my heart was pounding like an Indian drum. As Zoll was dependent on me to know how to act in the show, so I was dependent on the Great One for my knowing. I must listen carefully so the thunder in my heart would not drown out the hearing I must do.

I had never seen so many people before in my nine years. I had not thought so many people existed! Zoll's eyes searched mine calmly as I led him to the little stall where we were to await our turn to go on stage. Father and Mother had understood why I wanted to be alone with my fire mate before this contest. They had wished us well and left to take seats in the front row of the auditorium.

While we waited I looked around at the other dogs and their masters. Most of the people were adults wearing beautiful clothes and jewelry. A few of the dogs looked more like fancy toys I had seen in store windows at Christmastime than real creatures. They had the advantage of city ways to make them clever in dress and manner, but Zoll and I had the beauty and silence of the forest we loved to give us strength. And we had our soul-fire, the happy assurance of all-oneness.

The show began and one by one the contestants were called to enter the ring on the other side of the auditorium. We could not see the stage, but we could hear the applause and the loudspeakers. At last we were called: "Yvonne Walakea Laiwa showing Zoll!"

"Pretend we are in the forest, Zoll," I spoke silently. "I am the tribal princess, and you are my wild pony." The joy of being together flowed through us as we ran on stage. I could hear the people in the audience catch their breath as Zoll paused motionless at my side. In my hand I carried the woven leash Father had made. Zoll was free. His only bond was the flame of love we shared. As I ran, Zoll ran. He was my shadow. I felt the crowd's response before I heard it. People stood up and cheered. It was no contest for Zoll. He was all I knew him to be, and now the people in the audience knew it too.

When the judges' decision was announced, Zoll and I were called back to stand in the winner's circle. Again the audience stood and applauded. That sound was like nothing I had heard before. It both thrilled and frightened me. Mother and Father were called to the stage to stand with Zoll and me for the local photographers. Then there were pictures of the judges handing me the envelope with the prize money. Next came long rows of people with eager hands wanting to touch Zoll and ask me questions. We both longed for air—the fresh, cool air of our forest—but we were trapped by the crowd.

At last the line of people thinned and Zoll and I slipped out the back door which led to the athletic field. How good it felt to run surrounded by fresh air and silence! I found a water faucet where Zoll and I drank eagerly. Then we ran again, letting the wind blow in our faces. We were at home again in the outdoors—alone, yet glorying in all-oneness. Somehow I could not shut out entirely the sound of the crowd's wild applause and the exciting feeling of victory. It was a strange excitement—not at all like the aliveness we felt as we ran together. It was like watching with fascination a bonfire. I felt drawn to this strange new attraction, even while it made me uneasy. But the thought of the prize money was sweet and good. It would buy many things.

Zoll and I ran until we were tired. Then I put the collar and leash on him and we started walking around the buildings to where our car was parked. Mother and Father were quietly waiting for us there. My brothers and sisters had walked to Main Street where other events of the festival were being held that afternoon. My parents were anxious to join them and urged Zoll and me to walk down too. They promised we would go home before dark. Besides, so many people had not had a chance to see Zoll up close, they said.

So Zoll and I followed Mother and Father

down Main Street. Everywhere there were people wanting to congratulate us and pet Zoll. My heart swelled as his beauty was admired. There was that strange feeling again—the mixture of pleasure and fear! It was as if my soul-fire had flamed out of control. Again I wondered if it would be possible to hear the Great One above the many voices talking to me at once. I longed for silence. Mother and Father seemed so caught up in the festivities that I knew we must wait until they were ready to go home. So we walked on, curiously drawn to the pressing crowd, yet at the same time wary of it.

Halfway down Main Street Mother and Father stopped to visit with friends. Zoll and I continued on, always surrounded by a circle of new admirers with eager hands and questions. All the way through the center of the city we walked, followed by a wave of recognition which swallowed us as soon as we stopped.

CHAPTER SEVEN

We were standing on a corner waiting for the lights to change so we could cross the street when I noticed a man and woman in a car looking at us intently. Something in their faces made me notice them — but then wasn't everyone looking at Zoll that day? When I crossed the street, they made a U-turn at the corner and pulled to the curb beside us. The street was too crowded to park, so the man stayed in the driver's seat while the woman jumped out and pushed her way toward us. She had large, blue eyes, and she was staring at Zoll.

"Where did you get this Saint Bernard, young lady?" she asked in a breathless voice.

It was a question many had asked me that day, but something in her tone made me look at her face. Her eyes were bright with excitement. They never left Zoll. I tried to walk on without answering, but the woman stood directly in my path, looking at me.

"Young lady, I want to know where you got this Saint," she repeated in a low, firm tone.

"He is mine," I said quickly, trying to push past her.

The woman placed a hand on Zoll's head and began fingering his ear. "But *where* did you get him?" she insisted. "Did you buy him?" Her fingers kept moving along Zoll's ear as she talked.

Something in her manner made my soul-fire flicker. I must run, I thought. My grip on the leash tightened. "Come, Zoll, come!" I called silently. Then I turned and ran. Zoll was at my side instantly.

"Wait. . .wait!" the woman called, trying to follow us through the crowd. But Zoll and I had run through the forest together many times, and now the people were as so many trees as we raced past them.

At the first corner, we turned down the side street. I could hear the woman's voice still calling after us. In the middle of the block Zoll and I turned down a one-way alley. Without looking back we ran on in a zigzag course, keeping away from Main Street but heading back toward the auditorium where our car was parked. At last I saw the athletic field up ahead. In a few minutes we had crawled through the hedge and threw ourselves down on the cool grass behind it.

Even if the woman tried to follow us in a car, I knew it would not be easy for her to find us here. As soon as I caught my breath, I led Zoll along the hedge toward the far side of the field where the buildings were located. Beyond the buildings was the parking lot. At the end of the hedge I found the water faucet, and we quenched our thirst. I could see our car parked across the empty lot. No one was in sight, so we raced to the car. I opened the back door and Zoll jumped in. I made him lie on the floor, then I climbed up on the back seat and lay down, pulling the door shut behind me.

We waited in silence, hearing nothing except an occasional car drive by the school. It seemed hours before my family returned. I thought of the Great One as I lay there. I remembered how Zoll and I had found each other, and how my soul-fire had flamed at Zoll's kiss. Whatever danger that woman meant to us, surely our all-oneness would protect us. And yet I could not stop my soul-fire from quaking as I recalled her eyes staring at Zoll and the tone of her voice as she demanded to know, "Where did you get that Saint?"

At last I heard my family talking as they approached the car. I sat up, but I kept Zoll down on the floor out of sight.

"There she is!" they cried as they saw me. "What are you doing here, Yvonne? Where's Zoll?

There was no time to answer before my brothers and sisters reached the car and opened the door. Zoll wagged his tail happily as they climbed in.

"What are you two hiding from?" Paul teased. "Too much fame?"

Mother and Father's eyes were asking the same thing as they faced me. I hesitated. What was I hiding from? The look in a woman's eyes? What could I say?

"What were you hiding from, Yvonne?" Mother repeated Paul's question as she slid into the front seat beside Father.

"People," I said, hoping she would ask no more.

I felt her glance at me, half-hidden behind Leona's shoulder.

"People!" Paul exclaimed. "Did they like Zoll so much they wanted to take him from you?"

His words struck me like sharp stones.

"Did you or Zoll do anything wrong?" Father asked as he started the car and drove off.

Was it wrong to run away from fear, I wondered? "We only ran back to the car," I said.

Again I could feel Mother's eyes on my face. She changed the subject and began talking about the festival. All the way home the family chattered about the day's events. The encounter with the woman on Main

Street had made me forget the prize money Zoll had won. Now I thought of his performance again, and the sweet sound of applause as we stood in the winner's circle. The memory made me feel better. I saw Father turn into the reservation road and knew we would be home soon. By the time he pulled the car to a stop in our driveway, my spirits had revived and I joined in the family's gaiety.

Even though it was almost dark, Mother gave me permission to take Zoll for a short run before supper. No one was hungry after a day of hot dogs and sodas, but Mother insisted on a bowl of soup for everyone.

Once in the forest, Zoll and I ran as we had never run before. There was little light, but our feet knew the trail as we sped up the canyon to our favorite spring. How the crowd would cheer if they could see him now, I thought! As we raced around trees and boulders the slanted rays of remaining sunlight streaked Zoll's coat like sparkles on a lake. Darkness was falling when we reached the spring. We stayed just long enough to drink the cool, sweet water before starting back. My heart was as light as my footsteps as we plunged down the canyon wall toward the flat land where the settlement of houses formed our reservation village. We could see smoke from the chimneys and lights flickering as we raced along the familiar trail which led to our driveway.

Then Zoll and I saw it at the same
time — Chief Garret's police car parked in front
of our house! I tried to think he had come
to congratulate Zoll and talk about the show.
I tried to believe that was why he was here.
But my soul-fire quivered as Zoll and I
walked to the doorway and paused.

I could hear voices inside, but they were
only muffled sounds. I had to go in and find
out. Zoll had no collar, so I placed my hand
on his ruff and opened the door. Together we
walked in. The voices in the kitchen stopped.
We had been heard. Why was it so quiet?
I felt a strong urge to turn and run. The
forest was not far away, and it was vast
and safe. Yet here in our kitchen I sensed
a danger I dared not imagine.

There was a murmur of voices and Mother
called, "Is that you, Yvonne?"

So we moved forward, Zoll pressed to my
side as if we were yoked. The kitchen door
was open. I saw Chief Garret's face,
unsmiling. Next to him sat a strange man,
and on the other side, the woman!

If I had ordered Zoll to heel he could not
have obeyed more perfectly. He was a frozen
figure by my side. There were strange feelings
written on my parents' faces. I looked at the
woman, but her eyes were on Zoll alone.
The silence lasted only a moment, yet it was
like a vast hollow pit into which I sank.

"Yvonne, this is Mr. and Mrs. Roman

Borgman from Oregon. They told me a story
I want you to hear," Chief Garrett said.
"Mr. and Mrs. Borgman, this is Yvonne
Laiwa and Zoll."

The couple acknowledged me with a nod.
The woman's eyes never left Zoll. She turned
to Chief Garret. "May I examine his ears
now?" she asked.

Chief Garret looked from me to my parents
before answering. "Perhaps it would be
better if you told your story to Yvonne first."

The woman's tense body slumped a little
as she and her husband began to talk. They
had a Saint Bernard kennel in Oregon. For
twenty-five years they had worked to perfect
their line of Saints and had won both national
and international recognition with their
champions. The year before they had
produced a litter of eight pups that were
exceptional. At six weeks of age, four of the
pups showed signs of being prize dogs
with almost perfect conformation, markings,
and size. Of the four, one male was the
most striking young Saint the Borgmans had
ever seen, showing the results of their long
years of careful and patient breeding. That
pup was stolen by a pair of dognappers traf-
ficking in champion stock. These two men
were later caught breaking into another
kennel. One of the men turned state's witness
and admitted taking the prize pup from the
Borgmans. This man first claimed the dog

67

was destroyed, but under direct questioning by Mrs. Borgman he had changed his story. He said the pup had been dumped over the California border along a deserted county road.

Even though the chances of the puppy's survival were remote, the Borgmans had never given up hope that their potential champion might have been found. Since that time they had attended even more dog shows than usual, hoping that if the prize pup had been picked up it would be shown. Mrs. Borman felt certain she could recognize any of the dogs from that special litter at any age. Besides, each litter was permanently identified with a tattoo recorded with the National Dog Registry. "Usually our pups are not marked until they are older," Mrs. Borgman explained, "but because another kennel in our area had been the victim of dognappers we had this special litter tattooed at six weeks."

"We were on our way home today after participating in a dog show in San Francisco," Mrs. Borgman finished the account. "I spotted this Saint a block away and knew at once he could be our stolen male. He was obviously not an ordinary dog, much less an ordinary Saint Bernard." She was speaking directly to me as she continued. "Believe me, the only reason we were not at the show here was because we didn't know about it. We haven't passed up any chance of finding that puppy. After you ran away from me this afternoon, we went to the police station. Even in a city of this size a Saint like that has to be known. When the chief told us your story, I was sure we had found our stolen pup. So here we are."

Mrs. Borgman turned to Chief Garret. "Now may I check his ears for our tattoo?"

Chief Garret turned to me. "How about it, Yvonne? Doesn't that sound fair to you?"

Neither Zoll nor I moved. "He is mine!" I declared.

"I doubt that very much, young lady," Mrs. Borgman snapped. "How could a . . . girl like you own a prize dog like this?"

I felt Mother's swift motion as she stepped to my side. "There is good reason why Yvonne has a dog like Zoll. She saved his life. What she did was honorable. And she will do the honorable thing now." Mother's voice was steady and strong as she turned to me. "Yvonne, if *you* had lost Zoll, wouldn't you want to find him at any cost?" She did not wait for my answer, for we both knew what it would be. "Mrs. Borgman is asking for the right to find her lost puppy—not just lost, but stolen."

Mother's words were right, but the look in Mrs. Borgman's eyes took my breath away. At last I forced myself to speak. "Zoll is mine.

69

How can he be hers, too?"

"I can't answer that," Mother admitted. "I can only remind you that what she is asking is right."

Father got up and walked to my side. His voice was low and solemn as he spoke. "Remember too, Yvonne, that it is the tradition of our people, who have preserved in their hearts the legend of the Great One, to do what is right. The memory of that tradition is alive in you, my daughter. You will hear and do what is right. It is in you to do so."

So with my parents by my side, I gave Mrs. Borgman permission to look for a tattoo on Zoll's ears. In an instant she was on her knees before Zoll, stroking his massive head with her slender white hands. There were tears in her eyes as she turned back one of his ears and ran her fingertips carefully through the hairs.

Zoll and I were like statues. His great plume tail was as still as my lips. Surely his soul-fire must be trembling as fearfully as was mine!

Then I saw Mrs. Borgman's face flush with excitement. Her voice was like that of a wild beast as she shouted, "Here it is! The tattoo! I've found it!"

My soul-fire died.

It was useless to argue with the Borgmans. The tattoo was all the evidence they needed.

They were willing to go to court if necessary to prove that Zoll had been stolen from their kennel and was their property.

"But Zoll is not property!" I cried. "He is my fire mate! He is a gift from the Great One!"

"My dear child, this dog *is* stolen property, and he does not belong to you, no matter how you think you got him," Mrs. Borgman insisted. "Nevertheless, we will pay you handsomely for the care you have given him. You have done a very fine job, considering your circumstances. We will pay you six hundred dollars as a reward for the year's board and keep. With that amount you can buy yourself another pedigreed dog, even a Saint Bernard if you prefer, a dog that will really belong to you. Or you can buy something for yourself—clothes, or... whatever. I think that is a generous reward."

Six hundred dollars! Even with the dead weight in my heart I realized what that amount meant. It was more than Father earned for a month's hard work. It was more money than I had ever dreamed of having. But could money take the place of my fire mate?

"We neither need nor want your money as a payment or a reward," Father was saying. "We only want what is right. If Zoll is worth six hundred dollars, then we will buy him from you for that amount."

How my breath caught in my throat at Father's words!

But Mrs. Borgman's response was equally quick. "Oh, no, Mr. Laiwa, this dog is not for sale at any price! I am only trying to be fair with your daughter. The pup's care is worth that to us, but he is not replaceable. What he means to us and to our kennel cannot be computed in dollars."

"Nor can what he means to our daughter," Father remarked. He was speaking the words in my heart which my lips could not express. "If it were not for Yvonne, Zoll would not be here for you to claim."

"That is true," Mrs. Borgman admitted, "but it is also true that if he had not been stolen from us, your daughter would not have found him in the condition he was left in. All that is past, however. What matters now is that we have found him and identified him and are claiming rightful ownership under the law. I hope you will take the money we are offering and make it much easier all around." She turned to her husband. "Please write Mr. Laiwa a check, dear."

Mr. Borgman reached for his checkbook, but Mother's words stopped him. "What about Zoll? Would you replace his bond of love for Yvonne with a check? Look at them. They breathe the same breath, they are so close."

"That is a shame," Mrs. Borgman agreed,

"but it is really not our fault. This is the sad case with stolen property. However, the pup is young. He will miss your daughter, but in time he will learn to love one of us in her place. We are also very close to our Saints, you see. They are far more than just dogs to us." Mrs. Borgman turned to Chief Garret. "I am sorry, but it is getting late and it is useless to discuss the matter any further. Legally the dog is ours and we are claiming him. This is our right, isn't it?"

Chief Garret nodded his head sadly to confirm her words. He turned to me. "I believe you could wait for a court order, but all you stand to gain might be a bill for an attorney's fees and a few days' delay. This was the chance you took in the beginning, Yvonne. You lost. . . and we share your loss. I'm sorry."

Mr. and Mrs. Borgman insisted on taking Zoll with them right then. They would probably show him in Portland the following week, they said. If we wanted to attend the show they would pay our expenses for the trip in addition to the check for his care. Father refused both offers.

Neither Zoll nor I had moved during the entire discussion. But when Mrs. Borgman came forward to put a leash and collar on him, Zoll shook off her hand and tried to hide between my legs as he had done when he was a small pup. I knew I should order

him to go yet I could not make myself
speak that word. Mr. Borgman took the
choker and leash from his wife and slipped
them deftly over Zoll's head. As I stood there
unmoving between Father and Mother, Zoll
was led away, whining and barking as I
had never heard him do before. Even after
the Borgmans' car started off, his deep barks
trailed sadly behind in the still night air.

I know no words to tell my feelings as
I was left standing without my fire mate. I
rushed to my room and threw myself on my
bed as the tears came. I forgot my Indian
heritage of hiding feelings behind a closed
face. I forgot the Great One who has ever
guarded the soul-fires of our people. I forgot
that the others in my family loved Zoll too
and were suffering with me. I only knew
that Zoll—my fire mate, who was to be mine
forever—now belonged to someone else.

CHAPTER EIGHT

*A*ll night long I cried. Both
Mother and Father came to
my side often as the dark
hours passed. Only once Father spoke. "Now
is the time for strength, not weakness,
Walakea. Mother and I urge you to be
strong."

In the morning school was not mentioned.
My brothers and sisters left me alone.
They understood my grief and shared it.
I heard the school bus coming and the noise
as the young from our row of houses
poured out for the ride to the city.

After Mother and I were left alone, she
brought food to my bed. I did not want to
hurt her, but my throat was too full of tears
to swallow. So I lay in my bed all day,
sometimes sleeping, sometimes crying. I
remembered the feel of Zoll's warm body by
my side. I remembered his big head on my

pillow and the way his tail pounded my
legs when it wagged. I could see him
running through our forest with the slanted
rays of sun turning his coat into a mantle
of light. I thought of nothing but Zoll,
going over and over in my mind our last
day together and wondering, "What if . . .?"

What if we had never left the safety of our
forest, would the Borgmans have found Zoll?
What if I had not taken him to the dog show,
nor let his beauty be applauded by the crowd,
nor walked down Main Street to share his
glory with the people? Would Mrs. Borgman
have spotted him deep in our forest, running
up the canyon wall to the headwater of the
spring? Yet if it was wrong to go to the show,
why did not the Great One stop us? Had I
not been listening? Hour after hour I stirred
the ashes of my soul-fire with questions
that had no answers.

That night Father insisted I come to the
table and have dinner with the family. I
obeyed, but my stomach would not hold
food, and I had to run from the table with
my hand over my mouth.

For a second night I lay in my bed,
wide-eyed and crying. Again Mother and
Father came to my side often. This time it
was Mother who spoke. "Remember,
Walakea, that you are an Indian child,
guarded and guided by the Great One. Let
that all-oneness shield your soul-fire now and

restore it." But I had no soul-fire. I had only
a cold lump of sadness where the warm
flame had been. How could I believe in all-
oneness when Zoll was gone? Still, I thought
of Mother's words when my grief was
strongest, and they helped me.

In the morning I heard Mother and Father
discussing if I should go to school. They
wanted me to eat first, but the food they
made me take would not stay down. Finally
Mother called the principal and told him I
was not well. She did not tell him what was
wrong, and he did not ask. Perhaps he knew.
Zoll had won the hearts of many people at
that show, and even in the city news of
the Borgmans' legal claim traveled fast.

On the third day I still was not better,
and the doctor was called to our house.
He was firm as he spoke to me. I turned
my face away so he would not see the fresh
tears waiting to fall. He left some medicine—
something to help me forget Zoll, he said.
Forget Zoll? I did not want to forget him,
and even if I did it would be like trying
to forget myself.

Mother's face was drawn with worry and
fatigue, for now she did not leave my side
even at night. Perhaps she was afraid I would
try to run after Zoll. And perhaps I would
have, if my body had not been so weak.

I do not know how many days I lay there.
Time was like a cloud I could not see through.

Over and over in my weakness I spoke Zoll's
name, not with my lips but with my thoughts
as he and I had communicated so easily all
those months together. And somehow I felt
the current of love between us flow, complete
the life cycle, and return to me. Then I would
speak his name silently again and reach out
for the fire mate I no longer had.

So through strong remembering I began
to feel the cold ashes of my soul-fire
stirring. Like a tender green shoot, something
within me turned naturally to the Great One
whose gift to me Zoll had been. I remembered
the suffering of my people and how they
had perfected the art of listening during their
saddest days. Even when the great silence
fell as they retreated to their reservations, our
tribes handed down from father and mother
to son and daughter the tradition of the Great
One and the sacred rite of listening. It is
in listening that memory lives, and it is in
remembering that life is renewed as an
endless cycle of knowing. This cycle or
circle was the all-oneness of the Great One.
No one could take it from me as long as
I remembered it. It was the gift of gifts.
I had found it that night under the stars
before I found Zoll. Now I recalled all this,
and even in my grief I said those painful
words, "Thank you!"

One morning soon after I had spoken
those sacred words, Mother carried me out to

the front yard and laid me on a thick blanket
in the warm sun. I had not been outdoors
since that day of the dog show when Zoll
and I had gone for a run before supper.

The warmth of the sun roused me. I looked
around. I could see the trees of the forest
in a faraway mist. My eyes began shedding
tears as if the beauty I saw was more
than they could bear.

"Zoll!" my heart called. Perhaps it was the
sight of the forest that affected me, because
he did not feel as far away any more.

"Zoll!" I called again, this time with my
voice. Even my ears were deceiving me, for
I thought I heard a muffled bark. Surely it
was my memory playing tricks on me, for
now I heard a motor racing to a stop. I must
be remembering the car speeding up the
highway that night, stopping by my hiding
place in the brush. I recalled vividly the two
men and the sack that was thrown almost
at my feet. I relived my fear as I untied
the sack and saw that great masked face
peer out at me. . . and then the kiss and my
soul-fire bursting into flame!

My eyes flew open. Mother was standing
over me. She was alone. Tears were streaming
down her cheeks. . . but she was smiling!
Smiling? Not just smiling, but laughing through
her tears! And there *was* a car pulling to a fast
stop in our driveway, a familiar police car!
And out of the car lunged a Saint Bernard!

At first I thought it was Zoll. But this dog was far too thin to be Zoll. His coat was dull and his body sagged. Yet he was coming toward me...and something was happening to my heart as he came...and to my soul-fire!

"Zoll!" I called out weakly. Then a great body bounded against mine and a soft muzzle pressed against my cheeks. A warm wet tongue was kissing my face. My soul-fire was blazing!

I was laughing and crying at once, trying to hold Zoll in my weak arms while he wiggled and bounded and twisted, bumping me with his head as he pressed his wet nose to my face and filling the morning stillness with deep, throaty barks. But how thin he was! Where was his flesh, his thick, silky coat?

I turned from Zoll and saw Mrs. Borgman and Chief Garret standing by Mother. No one had dry eyes, but there were smiles shining through the tears like rainbows after a storm.

"What happened to Zoll?" I asked, looking from Mrs. Borgman to Chief Garret and back again.

Mrs. Borgman came and knelt beside Zoll and me. "My dear child," she began, "what has happened to *you*?"

I glanced at my arm across Zoll's ruff and realized I must look as thin as he did.

"I am so sorry, Yvonne," Mrs. Borgman

continued. "I was mistaken. Zoll *is* your dog—not ours. Legally he belonged to us, but there was a higher law that proved he really belonged to you. Zoll is your fire mate forever, just as you said." Her slim hand patted Zoll's lean frame as she told how he had cried day and night, refusing to eat until they feared for his life. So she had brought him back, driving all the way by herself while Mr. Borgman stayed behind at the kennel.

"I stopped at the police station to tell Chief Garret I was bringing Zoll back to where he belonged. That's when he told me about you. He asked if he could drive us up here so he could be in on this reunion." Chief Garret nodded in agreement. "I only hope I'm not too late," Mrs. Borgman finished. "Zoll is just a shadow . . . and you! If I had only known you were ill!"

"Me, ill?" I laughed. "I am not ill. I am only hungry!"

It was not many days after Mrs. Borgman returned to Oregon that Zoll and I were strong enough to walk to the edge of our forest together. Soon we were running, visiting our spring, renewing our friendship with the wild animals, and letting the warmth of our soul-fire touch all we saw. The luster came back to Zoll's coat and the sure swiftness returned to his legs. He was my Indian pony again and I his princess Walakea.

Mother's eyes lost their tired look, and Father stood taller and straighter than ever before. Even my brothers and sisters seemed closer to me, as if through the trial of my soul-fire they had become aware of their own inner flame and the need to find its Source.

Now Zoll and I are in our third year together. The Borgmans come to visit us often on their way to and from their kennels. On one of their trips they brought with them a beautiful female Saint Bernard. Soon Zoll will have a pup of his own to teach, and someday I too must pass on the gift of all-oneness I know. Until then there is still much listening I must do.

I-Yvonne have spoken long enough. Come, Zoll! Come, fire mate! Let us run in our forest together where the silence is vast, for the Great One is waiting to be heard. I-Walakea go to listen!

PHOTOGRAPHS

Kimberlee Laiwa, ten years old, is the girl
pictured on the cover. Kimberlee is a Pomo
Indian; she lives on the Manchester Point
Arena Rancheria at Point Arena. Kimberlee
does Indian dancing. Her parents, Ken and
Shirlee Laiwa, are active in preserving and
restoring Indian customs and heritage.

Of the St. Bernards who modeled for Zoll,
the star is Amy, officially Belyn's Amanda
Von Senino. Her owners are Peter and Kathy
Bishop of Gualala, California.
Other models include St. Bernards bred
and raised by the Cossis in Gualala.

ABOUT THE AUTHOR

Olga Cossi

Ms. Cossi is a resident of Gualala,
California. She was graduated from the
Palmer School of Authorship in Los Angeles.
Her experience in the field of journalism is
wide; she has been a staff correspondent
for the *Santa Rosa Press Democrat* and a
columnist for the *Mendocino Beacon.* She is
a member of the Society of Children's Book
Writers and a free-lance writer. For the past
four years Ms. Cossi has been "on a sab-
batical from free-lancing to do an in-depth
study I call linguistic archaeology. From this
have evolved four books, one of them
Fire Mate." When asked her reasons for writ-
ing *Fire Mate,* Ms. Cossi replied, "I have
always felt a closeness to the Indians whose
appreciation for the outdoors my St. Bernards
and I shared. The deep woods became the
hearth for my soul-fire. Here the girl-child
within me found her fire mate. I knew
someday I would have to write this story."